Another Sommer-Time Story™

MAYOR
FOR A DAY

by Carl Sommer
Illustrated by Dick Westbrook

DISCARD

Advance · HOUSTON
PUBLISHING, INC

Permissions
Advance Publishing, Inc.
6950 Fulton St.
Houston, TX 77022

www.advancepublishing.com

First Edition
Printed in Singapore

Library of Congress Cataloging-in-Publication Data

Sommer, Carl, 1930-
   Mayor For A Day / by Carl Sommer; illustrated by Dick Westbrook, -- 1st ed.
    p. cm. -- (Another Sommer-Time Story)
   Summary: When he gets to be mayor of his small, peaceful town for a day, Davy decides to abolish all rules–which turns out to be a big mistake.
   Cover title: Carl Sommer's Mayor For A Day.
   ISBN 1-57537-013-1 (hardcover; alk. paper). -- ISBN 1-57537-057-3 (library binding :alk. paper).
   [1. Conduct of life Fiction. 2. Behavior Fiction. 3. City and town life Fiction.] I. Westbrook, Dick, ill. II. Title. III. Title: Carl Sommer's Mayor For A Day. IV. Series: Sommer, Carl, 1930- Another Sommer-Time Story.
PZ7.S696235May 2000   99-35276
[E]--dc21   CIP

MAYOR
FOR A DAY

It was the first game of the season for the Cougars. Nearly everyone in Springdale came to cheer the junior soccer team.

Even the mayor was there! He said to the players, "If the Cougars win the championship, the team's best player will become mayor for a day."

No one gave much thought to what the mayor had said—including the mayor. Small, peaceful Springdale never had a winning team.

However this year, the Cougars beat every team they played, even teams from the big cities. And no one played better than Davy. He ran fast and kicked hard.

But to win the championship, the Cougars had to beat the undefeated Riverdale Lions. Riverdale was a large town, and for the last three years the Lions had won the championship.

Because the Lions always had the best team, everyone was certain they would win again, especially against small, peaceful Springdale.

In the championship game, the Cougars scored four goals—Davy made two himself. But the Lions fought back to tie the score. Now the Cougars were down to their last play. Davy ran down the field, tapping the ball and scooting around two players. With ten seconds left, Davy kicked the ball hard—right into the corner of the net!

The Cougars won the game! The crowds stood and cheered, "Cougars! Cougars! Number one! Cougars! Cougars! Number one!"

And Davy was chosen, "Most Valuable Player!"

Mary said to Davy, "You were great! We're all excited that on Saturday we'll be going to the town square for the victory celebration, and *you're* going to be mayor for a day. What are you going to do when you're the mayor?"

"Hmmm," said Davy. "I don't know."

His friends told him what they would do if they were mayor for a day:

"Have an ice cream party where you can eat all you want!" said Jesse.

"Close the schools for the *whole* day!" suggested Tammy.

"Make it a 'Fun Day'—No work allowed!" said Brian.

When Davy came home, Dad said, "I'm proud of you. You played a great game."

"Me too," said Mom. "I've cooked a special meal and baked your favorite dessert."

When Davy saw the cake, he said, "Mmmmm! Mmmmm! I just want to eat dessert."

"You know the rules," said Dad. "No dessert until you eat your meat and vegetables."

Yes, Davy knew the rules, but to him there were too many:

Look both ways before crossing the street.
Go to bed on time.
Sit up straight.
Eat your food.
Brush your teeth.
Clean your room.
Make your bed.
Do your homework.
"Whew!" Davy mumbled to himself. "I hate rules!"

When Dad heard his mumbling, he said, "A family without rules will never be happy."

"I don't think so," thought Davy. "If we didn't have rules, then we'd *really* be happy."

After supper, Davy always had to do his homework. If he finished early, he could go outside and play.

But today, instead of doing his homework right away, Davy watched his friends play. Then he groaned, "Ohhhhh! How I wish I didn't have to do my homework."

By the time he decided to do his homework, it was getting late. He would not finish his homework until bedtime. Davy sat at his desk and complained, "Why do *I* always have to go to bed so early? Rules, rules, rules! I'd be happy to have just *one* day without any rules!"

On Saturday the whole town came out to
honor Davy and the championship team. The
band played and the people cheered. Davy led
his team at the front of the parade.

When they reached the town square, the
mayor hushed the crowd. "On Monday," he
proclaimed, "Davy will be mayor for a day!"

"Hooray!" everyone shouted.

Then the mayor said, "Davy, what do you

want? An ice cream party? A fun day? The town is yours. You can do whatever you want."

The band leader raised his baton, the drummers lifted their sticks, the horn-blowers drew a deep breath. Everyone waited. A great hush fell over the crowd.

Then Davy announced with a great big smile and a loud voice, "On Monday—there will be no rules!"

"No rules?!!!" gasped the mayor.

"Hoorayyyyy!!!" shouted all the boys and girls.

"Ohhhhhh!!!" groaned all the dads and moms. They knew that a day without rules would be a great disaster.

The mayor now realized how foolish he had been for making such a promise. But he had given his word, and a promise is a promise.

The mayor bowed his head and said, "I must honor my word. On Monday, we will have no rules."

"Hoorayyyyy!!!" yelled all the boys and girls. They jumped up and down and shouted, "Monday will be our best day ever!"

When Davy walked into the kitchen Monday morning, he announced, "Mom, I don't want to eat breakfast today."

"But you're going to be hungry," warned Mom.

"I'll be all right," said Davy.

"Okay," said Mom.

"Wow!" whispered Davy. "This is going to be a great day!"

As Davy went to walk out the door, he said, "I don't want to wear my jacket to school."

"You better wear it," advised Dad. "You'll be cold."

"I'll be all right," said Davy.

"Okay," answered Dad.

"Hooray!" yelled Davy. "This is how it should *always* be. I can do whatever *I* want!"

While waiting for the school bus, Davy felt cold—so cold he began to shiver. "Brrrrrr, I'm freezing!" he told his friend. "I should have worn my jacket."

While sitting at his desk, Davy became so hungry that his stomach began to growl and hurt.

"I'm starving," he whispered to the boy in front of him. "I wish it were lunchtime."

"It's two hours until lunchtime," said the boy.

"Two hours?" moaned Davy. "I wish I had eaten breakfast."

"R-r-r-r-r-ring!" sounded the school bell.

"Finally!" sighed Davy. "It's lunchtime."

The students jumped up and ran to the lunchroom. Only Davy and two other kids waited for the teacher to dismiss them.

"What's going on?" Davy asked the teacher.

He was so hungry and eager for the lunchtime bell, that he had forgotten what he had done.

"Remember?" the teacher reminded him. "Today, we have no rules in our school."

"That's right!" said Davy as he jumped out of his chair. "This is going to be a g-r-e-a-t day."

As soon as Davy walked into the hall, a boy ran into him and knocked him down.

"Ouch!" yelled Davy as he hit his head against the wall.

Davy rubbed his head and complained, "Why are teachers letting kids run in the halls?"

Then he remembered that there were no rules today. "I should have kept one rule—'No running in the halls.'"

Since Davy had skipped breakfast, he could hardly wait to eat. While standing in the lunch line, a group of boys jumped in front of him.

"Hey!" complained Davy. "Why don't you guys go to the back of the line?"

"Because we don't have to," said the big kid.

"That's not fair!" said Davy.

"Try to stop me," the big kid snapped back.

Davy knew he could not stop him. The boy was bigger and stronger than he was.

Davy said to the girl behind him, "I should have kept the rule—'No cutting in line.'"

As the day wore on, more and more kids remembered that *today* there were no rules.

Kids began climbing on desks and flying paper airplanes, throwing erasers and shooting rubber bands, yelling and chasing each other—

all in the classroom!

At first, Davy joined in. He thought it was fun. But the fun quickly wore off when some kids got mad and began fighting. And no one stopped them—they did as they pleased.

For the rest of the class, Davy sat in his chair with a big frown on his face.

Then a shoe hit him in the head. "Ouch!" he yelled. "I should have kept *all* the school rules!"

Finally, the last bell rang and school was over. Everyone, especially Davy, was glad to be going home.

Davy said to a friend, "That was the worst school day ever! A school without rules is terrible!"

Davy was glad to be home again. He sat down and began doing his homework. Suddenly he threw up his hands and shouted, "Oh good! Today I don't have to do my homework!"

He jumped up, grabbed a soccer ball, and headed straight to his friend's house.

"Look both ways before you cross the street!" Mom called.

"Mom must have forgotten," thought Davy. "That's a rule, and today there are no rules!"

Davy never even bothered looking as he began crossing the street.

Zoommmmm!!!! went a car as it raced down the street. Davy jumped back onto the sidewalk, barely getting out of the way!

"Hey!" shouted Davy. "You're going much too fast! I could have been killed!"

"No rules today!" yelled the driver as he sped out of sight.

Davy was so scared that he shook all over as he walked to his friend's house.

After hearing what had happened, his friend reminded him, "Davy, did you forget that today people can drive any way they want?"

Davy mumbled to himself, "I should have kept the driving rules."

Then Davy said to his friend, "Come on, let's have some fun and play ball."

They met some friends and began playing soccer. The ball came to Davy, but before he could kick it, someone pushed him down.

"Hey!" yelled Davy. "That's not fair!"

"No soccer rules today," snapped the kid.

A few minutes later, Davy had a chance to score a goal. But when he kicked the ball hard to the goal, a player jumped up in the air and caught the ball. Then he ran away with it.

"What are you doing?" shouted Davy. "That's not the way to play the game!"

"I don't care," yelled the kid. "That's the way *I* want to play. Remember? No rules today!"

Then the other boys began breaking the rules. It was the worst game of soccer that Davy had ever played. Davy went home mad. Today, he did not even have fun playing his favorite game.

Meanwhile, all around town, people were becoming very angry with Davy. Without any rules, their small town was anything but peaceful. People were yelling:

"Stop stealing!"

"Get off the road!"

"You're driving too fast!"

To some people, "no rules" meant they could do—and have—whatever they wanted.

In stores, sales people were selling, but buyers were not buying. They were taking items off the shelves and walking out the store!

In restaurants, cooks were cooking, but people were not paying for the food they ate! Things were getting worse and worse.

Angry men and women and boys and girls began gathering in the town square.

"It's all Davy's fault!" they complained.

"That's right," yelled someone in the crowd. "This was a peaceful town until *he* became mayor!"

More and more people kept coming until nearly the whole town showed up.

Even the real mayor was there!

"This is no way to run a town!" an angry woman shouted. "This madness must stop!"

"It will," answered the mayor, "tomorrow when we get our rules back!"

"Tomorrow will be too late!" roared the crowd.

Someone yelled out, "Let's find Davy! It's all his fault!"

"Yes!" screamed the mob. "Let's go!"

Everyone began marching toward Davy's house.

Davy had no idea what was happening in the town square. When he came home from playing soccer, he looked into the pot of food that Mom was cooking, and groaned, "I don't want to eat that."

"But it's good for you," said Mom.

"Remember?" said Davy. "No rules today."

"What do you want?" asked Dad.

Davy rubbed his stomach. "I want a large bowl of ice cream with lots of fudge topping covered with cherries!"

"You won't feel good if you eat only that," warned Dad.

"I'll be all right," said Davy with a big grin.

"Okay," answered Dad.

"Mmmmm!!!! Mmmmm!!!!" mumbled Davy. He ate and ate and ate. It was his best meal ever! "This is the way we should *always* eat!"

Then Davy smiled and said, "Maybe the day will turn out just fine after all."

As soon as Davy had finished eating, his stomach began to hurt real bad. He decided to go to bed.

"Ohhhhhh!!!!" he groaned over and over again. "My stomach hurts. I wish I hadn't eaten all that ice cream!"

As Dad and Mom sat next to Davy trying to comfort him, they heard a loud noise. Dad rushed to the window.

"What's happening?" asked Mom.

"Uh, oh!" said Dad shaking his head. "It's the mayor and the whole town! We're in big trouble."

"Get Davy out here!" demanded the mob.

Davy felt so bad that he could barely get out of bed. He held his stomach as he walked to the front door.

As soon as Dad opened the door, someone yelled at Davy, "You've ruined our town!"

"What do you mean?" asked Davy.

The mayor told him about all the trouble that they were having. Then he said, "You cannot have a town without rules."

Davy knew all too well what he meant—and he knew how to fix it.

"I'm sorry," said Davy to the crowd. "I thought a day without rules would be the happiest day of my life—but this has been the WORST day of my life! Now I know that rules are very, very important."

Then Davy looked at the Mayor and said, "Mr. Mayor, you are right. You cannot have a town without rules."

Then he turned around and said, "And Dad, you are right, too. A family without rules will never be happy."

Then turning to the crowd, Davy said, "From this moment on, I am no longer the mayor. I resign!"

Everyone clapped and shouted, "Hooray!"

They lifted Davy onto their shoulders. Davy had never felt better—stomachache and all.

Then the mayor cleared his throat and announced, "As mayor of this fine community, I declare that from now on—we have rules!"

"Hooray!!!" shouted the crowd. And Davy shouted the loudest of all.